Boo Boo La Roo

by Diana Howard

Illustrated by Harris H. Huber

Book Design by Tad Roberts

Published by BookLocker.com, Inc., St. Petersburg, Florida.

Printed on acid-free paper.

Booklocker.com, Inc. 2021

This is the story of Boo Boo La Roo,
a tiny, audacious Elephant Shrew.

He is soft. He is quick.
He makes nary a sound,
yet his need to be daring
is ALWAYS around.

3

Why just last week he heard Mama declare
his fiftieth march to the time out lair.

4

At lunch today
Dada scolded so sternly,
"Boo Boo you're testing
my patience quite firmly.

Spiders are yummy can you not see,
if you take three bites
how pleased we will be?"

"Three bites of Spider?"
Boo Boo lamented.

"Son," said Dada,
"when you're up to the job
of eating your spiders
without a sob,

8

then wipe that
floppity frown
off your face,
hop down from that rock
and sit at your place."

9

Yet Boo Boo's big ears
didn't work as they should

because HE heard Dada
tell Mama he COULD...

go for a ride on a crocodile's tail,

flapping his elephant ears like a sail,

or swing with a monkey
from branch to branch,

high in the air through
the trees they would dance.

15

You know that a shrew
like Boo Boo LaRoo
will ALWAYS want
something clever to do.

Like using his feet
(they are long like his nose)

to pounce on his brother.
Look out! Here he goes.

17

It's fun for a bit
though soon brings a scowl
'cause Mamas don't like it
when wee ones howl.

"What did I do?" Boo Boo asked with a blink.
"What did I do to cause such a stink?"

18

Back to his rock
Boo Boo went with a pout.
"It just isn't fair,"
he cried with a shout!

19

He laid on his back, his head upside down.
He said to himself, "There's no need to frown.

I get it. I know what rules are about.
I see it so clearly without any doubt.

It's about eating spiders
chewy and green,

about licking my paws
until they are clean,

about listening closely to know what's right,
about using manners and being polite."

Boo Boo jumped down
with a look that was meek.

He ran to Mama
who nuzzled his cheek.

Dada was there with a wink in his eye.

He said to his son with a patient sigh,

"Boo Boo La Roo, come and sit by our side.
We see that you hear and know that you try

to follow our rules
and do what is right
yet still have some mischief
to bring you delight.

27

Take turns with your brothers.
Be thoughtful and kind.
Eat all your green spiders,
and then you will find

that magically trials and trouble and sad
will turn into happy and jolly and glad."

This book is dedicated to
Porter, Reed, and Luke.

A special thank you to
Tad Roberts
for his patience with and dedication to
the graphic design of this project.

CPSIA information can be obtained
at www.ICGtesting.com
Printed in the USA
BVHW062058290821
615283BV00001B/2